THE TWELVE DAYS OF CHRISTMAS:
A TALE OF CHRISTMASTIDE.
WITH ELVES.

THE TWELVE DAYS OF CHRISTMAS: A TALE OF CHRISTMASTIDE. WITH ELVES.

A. M. Offenwanger

amovitam press

This is a work of fiction. Names, characters, places, and events are either the products of the author's imagination or used in a fictitious manner. Any resemblance to actual persons or events, living or dead, is purely coincidental (especially in the case of dead events).

amovitam press

ISBN 978-1-988273-06-8

THE FIRST DAY OF CHRISTMAS

If you think that elves are small, cute, cheerful creatures with pointy ears, green hats, and jingle bells on the hems of their shirts, do yourself a favour: *think again*. Mind you, I can understand how you would come to such a conclusion, especially at this time of year—even our small town has a Santa in front of the grocery store with those little green guys flocking around him, luring small children to sit on his knee. Luring them—that's about the only way in which the cheesy Christmas elves resemble the real thing.

I don't know if it would have helped Tom any if he had known what elves are really like, that Christmas Eve he disappeared.

Tom Rimer is—well, was—my boyfriend. We had made tentative plans for him to pick me up from my place so we could go up the valley to spend Christmas Eve with my family; on Christmas Day he was on the early shift in Lord's Mine.

He didn't show up. I wasn't too surprised—Tom's a good guy, but not the most punctual; he tends to lose track of time.

However, when half an hour after he was supposed to have been there he was still a no-show with no communication on whether he was coming or not, I was getting a little miffed. After an hour, I was fuming. I'd tried calling him about three times, but the cell reception isn't the best around here, so I didn't get through.

I reached for my phone one more time and was just starting to type out yet another irate message, when my phone pinged and a text from Tom popped up on my screen.

"*12 days xmas*" it said, "*has 2B the whole thi*"

"**thing*"

"*else I'm stuck here*"

"*pls try!!!*"

Say what? Tom is prone to being cryptic with his texting, but this was a bit much.

"*???*" I texted back, then, "*Where r u?*"

But there was no response—it was almost like I could hear the texts falling into the silence of an empty room. I gave up.

"*Leaving without you,*" I texted, "*c u Saturday*"

The next afternoon—Christmas Day—was when it started up.

"Look at this, Mac," my mom called out, "come over here!"

I stepped over next to her by the living room window and looked out into the snow-covered yard.

The Bosc pear tree still had a few forlorn brown fruits dangling from its highest branches where Dad hadn't been able to reach them—plus, he always said, leave some for the critters, they need to live too.

In this case it looked like the critter in question was a small, round bird, perched on the spreading lower branches of the tree.

"That's a big quail," I said. "I didn't know they like sitting in trees. And where's the rest of the flock?"

"It's not a quail," Mom said, "it's a partridge. Get it?"

Oh, cute. A partridge in a pear tree.

I reached for my cell, shook it to open the camera—it's one of the features I like about that phone—snapped a picture, and texted it to Tom along with a pointed "*See what you're missing?*"

I never got a response, but as I figured he was at work I wasn't too worried. Unfortunately.

When I got home late that night, I found a message on the answering machine of my landline.

"Hey, this is Herb. Trying to get a hold of Tom; he didn't show up for work today. Tell him to get in touch, would you?"

THE SECOND DAY OF CHRISTMAS

I went over to Tom's house first thing in the morning on Boxing Day, before it was even light—not that that means much this time of year; sunrise doesn't come until almost nine o'clock. His truck wasn't parked at the curb where he usually leaves it. I used the key he'd hidden on top of the lintel—he figured that was safer than under the door mat—and let myself into his basement suite.

There was no sign of Tom. The bed looked slept in, but that didn't mean anything—he never made it, so it always looked slept in. The real clue was the coffee maker. The dregs in the bottom were stone-cold, so he definitely had not been home that morning; he would never leave the house without at least one cup of fresh-brewed coffee.

A while ago, he had been making some vague noises about going ice fishing on Boxing Day with a buddy—I couldn't remember who—but surely he would at least have let me know?

I checked the time on my phone. Seven thirty—I could probably get away with going upstairs to talk to his landlady.

"No, haven't seen Tom," Lilian, who was still in her housecoat, said cheerfully. "Not since Christmas Eve morning. But guess what I did see?" Suddenly she gasped. "There! There they are again!" She rushed towards her patio door, then stopped a few feet short of it and crept slowly closer, waving at me to follow.

"Look!" she whispered, pointing out the door. "A pair of turtle doves!"

Through the door I could hear the distinctive hooting call of the grey-brown birds that were perched on the edge of Lilian's bird feeder. I knew that hoot well, as Tom liked to copy it—he could make all sorts of noises by blowing into his cupped hands. He tried to teach me, but I could never pull it off. I have to stick with beatboxing, which I'm not too bad at, even if I do say it myself.

"I saw them yesterday, during the Christmas bird count!" Lilian said, enraptured. "They don't usually stay around for the winter, but this year they did! They're so beautiful! I had to list them as mourning doves, of course; that's what they insist on calling them in the records—but my family's always called them turtle doves. Two turtle doves—that's really unusual this time of year. Maybe I'll win birder of the month with that!"

"Nice," I said, pulled out my phone and shook it to open the camera. Even in the low early morning light the birds came out clearly in the photo; that could be nice on Instagram. "So, look," I said, "could you do me a favour and let me know if you hear from Tom?"

"Oh, sure." She nodded, her dyed red curls bobbing. "Maybe that lady out at Carson's Landing knows something; I think that's who he was talking to Tuesday morning."

"What lady?"

Her eyes were back on the birds out on the patio, and she answered absentmindedly.

"Oh, you know, that sexy one in the fancy new house they built at Jimbo Carson's old place. Her and Tom were standing out by the street, and Tom looked real smitten with her. Oops—I didn't mean…" She looked around at me and giggled sheepishly. "I'm sure he isn't—didn't—"

No, probably not. Tom wouldn't cheat on me—would he?

THE THIRD DAY OF
CHRISTMAS

Mary-Lou didn't think so either when I talked to her. We have an affinity—we bonded over both of us being named Mary-Something. My full name is Mary-Claire, which I think makes me sound like either a Southern belle or a Catholic nun. Fortunately nobody but my grandmother has ever called me anything but the short version.

"No, Mac," said Mary-Lou, who had known Tom all his life. "He's not a cheat. He won't pull an Eldon; the only vanishing tricks he does are slight-of-hand in his magic shows."

"Pulling an Eldon"—now there's a local phrase for you. Until Mary-Lou said it, I hadn't even realized that that's what I was worried about. It referred to Eldon "Elvis" Lynn, who disappeared in 1971, which his old girlfriend Celia Whitewell would tell anyone who was willing to listen and a few other people besides. The town thought that most likely he'd just run off with another woman; there were rumours of a pretty blonde he'd been seen with just before he vanished. And as he'd been an Elvis impersonator—his party piece that year being Elvis' new release "I'll Be Home on Christmas Day"—he'd had his fair share of groupies. But Celia wasn't having any of it. It was kind of sad: nearly fifty years later she was still waiting for Eldon to come back, kept doing her now-grey hair in a Priscilla Presley style because she thought he would like it, and wouldn't hear a word against him. He was kidnapped, she insisted. By what—aliens? This time of year she always got worse than usual because it was around Christmas that he'd vanished. She should really just accept that Eldon had left her and skipped town.

But then... For the first time I got an inkling of where she was coming from. I still hadn't heard from Tom, and it was now going on three days.

"Are you sure Tom hasn't just gone AWOL or something?" I said.

"Sure I'm sure," Mary-Lou said comfortably. "I've known the guy since Kindergarten, remember."

We were out in her barn, where she was feeding her chickens. Mary-Lou collects fancy breeds of farmyard fowl.

"Why do you think he hasn't texted?" I said, absentmindedly staring at a fat white chicken. It had a brown back that had the most comical ruff of feathers around its neck, like people in seventeenth-century paintings, and even funnier "socks" on its feet, as if it was wearing pants with long lace cuffs peeping out of the leg bottoms.

"Oh, you know him. Communication isn't his strong suit." Mary-Lou scattered another handful of chicken feed, and two more of those funny-looking chickens with the neck ruffs came running up, clucking madly. Mary-Lou chuckled at the sight of them. "Those are my newest girls," she said proudly. "I got them for Christmas. They're Faverelles; it's a French breed—supposed to be good layers." She checked the level of water in the watering dish. "Didn't you say Tom did send you a text?"

"Just the once, on Christmas Eve, but I can't make heads or tails of it." I pulled my phone out of my pocket, thumbed open the message, and held it out to her.

She took a look and shook her head. "No, makes no sense to me either," she said. "Maybe he meant that he's going to be gone for twelve days this time?"

"Maybe." I pulled my shoe out of the way of the pecking beak of one of Mary-Lou's fancy new beruffled chickens. "I just wish he'd have said so." Now all three of the French hens were clustered around my feet. I turned on the phone camera and snapped a photo; they were such funny-looking things.

Suddenly my phone buzzed in my hand. Tom!
"*pls keep tryi*"
"*I lv u*"
What on earth was going on?

9

THE FOURTH DAY OF CHRISTMAS

I couldn't get through to Tom. None of my texts got a response. I had to go back to work on the 28th, so I didn't have time to go running around looking for him. I'd stopped in at the police station on the way home from Mary-Lou's to at least ask what it takes to file a missing person report, but they'd already shut up shop for the weekend.

And besides, Tom was supposed to be at work in the mine, right? I tried to call Herb, the foreman, but couldn't get a hold of him. I told myself that the fact that he hadn't called back about Tom not showing up was a good sign. But just on the off-chance that Lilian had heard something, I dropped by her place in the afternoon when I got off work.

"Bohemian waxwings!" she greeted me by the

door. "Just imagine!"

I was a little taken aback. Bohemian what?

"At my feeder!" Lilian gushed. "This morning!"

Oh. More birds.

"That's nice," I said. "Have you heard from Tom?"

"No, why?" She didn't even pause for me to answer. "If I don't get Birder of the Month for this… They were sitting there, one on either side of the feeder, calling to each other! That's what tipped me off; they sound really different from, say, the Cedar waxwings! Here, look—" She picked up her little point-and-shoot digital camera. "I took a video!"

She brought up her picture gallery and booted up the video. It showed a couple of sleek, taupe-coloured birds with blush-red faces, bars of black streaking back from the beaks over their eyes to the funny little crests on the tops of their heads. They flapped their black-and-yellow-tipped wings at each other and chirped, hopping back and forth.

"They were right here!" Lilian said, pulling me by the sleeve over to the patio door. "See, there—" She gave a little scream. "They're here again! Look, just look! There's *four* now! I've never, never…" She was practically hyperventilating.

It was pretty cool, I had to admit. The birds were even more beautiful in real life than on her little video, and she was right, they sat there calling out to each other, almost like they were having a conversation. I took a quick picture on my phone, and caught them just as they took flight. Yes, I'd got them all in the frame.

But there had been something… "Could I see your video again for a minute?"

"Sure. Aren't they gorgeous?" Lilian handed me her camera.

There! That's what it was—there was a person in the background of her little movie! Kind of blurry and small, just visible through the slats of her patio railing—it looked like a woman with long blonde hair. I didn't recognize her, but she was staring at the house with a strange expression on her face. Greedy.

"Who's this?" I rewound the video clip a bit and set it playing again. "There, that person in the background?"

Lilian took the camera out of my hand and peered at the screen at arm's length. "Can't say I... Wait a moment!" She picked up her reading glasses, which hung on a chain around her neck, and perched them on her nose. "Ah! Kind of hard to see, but that's that lady Tom was talking to a couple of days ago. You know, the one from out at—"

"—at Carson's Landing, yes, I remember." Maybe it was time to contact this woman, after all. She was the last person I knew for a fact had talked to Tom. And that look on her face, in spite of the blurriness of the image, sent a shiver down my spine.

THE FIFTH DAY OF CHRISTMAS

I had to work again the next day. Usually I turn off my phone while I'm working; it's not cool to have the phone ringing while you're talking to a customer or, worse, while you're measuring out pills for a prescription. Pharmacy techs can't afford to get distracted. But that day, I kept the phone on.

Still no word from Tom.

To distract myself from my—well, I wouldn't say worries, but let's call them *concerns*, I stopped in at Engelhard's on the way home from work. Engelhard's is a clockmaker's and jeweller's. That's right, even in a town so small that our shopping is restricted to a grocery store, a drug store and a second-hand book shop, we have our very own jeweller. Old Mr. Engelhard came over from "ze Old Vorld", as he was fond of pointing out, where he properly learned his trade "back in ze olden days". Now the shop is run by Young Mr. Engelhard, or, as everyone calls him, Joe, who is about sixty-five. But for all he keeps up his father's old-world business practises, he added on the tech savvy of a much younger man. Among other things, he's expanded the shop into an online mail-order business, and he is servicing people's cuckoo clocks from as far away as Toronto. He loves his work so much, he's even there on a Sunday—only open for six hours, though, which counts as downright slacking off for him.

What drew me to Engelhard's was, I'm embarrassed to say, the rings. For a while now, I'd been eyeing up their selection of engagement rings. I'd never actually gone so far as to bring Tom into the store to show him—I'm not quite that un-subtle—but there's no harm in dreaming, is there?

However, it had been a mistake to look at the rings that day. All it did was to keep Tom at the forefront of my mind, which was exactly the opposite of what I was trying to do.

I let me eye travel over the familiar contents of the glass case. But wait—not all of it was familiar! It seemed that over Christmas, Joe had brought in a couple of new rings. There they were, sparkling against the black velvet of the display: five classic gold rings, the diamonds glittering in their settings. I pulled out my phone. "Do you mind?" I asked Joe, gesturing with the phone.

"No, no, you go right ahead. Make sure you tag us on Facebook if you post the picture."

I chuckled. "I'll be sure to do that," I said and snapped the photo. "You've sold the princess-cut, I see."

"Yes, I did that. Just before Christmas, it was."

"Who to, I wonder?"

Joe smiled. "Now that would be telling," he said with a wink.

Oh. Did he mean…?

No. No, this wasn't helping. I had to get my mind off Tom.

The bell over the door of the shop tinkled, and Joe and I both turned to see who had come in. My jaw dropped. The guy who walked into the store was the most handsome man I had ever seen. Dark hair like Tom's crisply curling back from his broad forehead; silver-grey eyes with laugh lines at the corners (except that he seemed too young to have lines in his face); high cheekbones and a jaw so chiselled it was downright stereotypical. He dusted fresh snow off his broad shoulders—was it snowing again?—then turned a blindingly white smile on me that made me go weak at the knees.

"Hi!" he said in a sonorous baritone, "I hear this is the place to get rings?"

"I, um, uh," I stuttered, my mouth dry. Then I pulled myself together and pointed at Joe. "Mr. Engelhard is the one to ask. I don't, uh, belong here."

"Ah. That, I find hard to believe. This is a place for beauty." The man gave me another dazzling smile.

"What can I do for you?" Joe put in.

I beat a retreat. What had come over me, going weak at the knees like that, staring at this guy? I'd seen handsome men before… But there was something about this one, something that drew me… Who *was* this man?

THE SIXTH DAY OF CHRISTMAS

I woke up the next morning with a start. What on earth had I been thinking? It was as if that gorgeous man in Engelhard's had literally driven Tom from my mind! I snatched up my phone from my bedside table and tried to turn it on. All I got was a blank screen. With a groan I realized I'd forgotten to charge it.

A couple of hours later I was at Mary-Lou's. "And even once it was charged there was nothing," I said to her. "I've gone and filed that missing persons report with the police. They said they'd let me know right away if anything turns up."

"Then that's what they'll do," Mary-Lou said. "But I'm sure Tom is fine; he usually is." She picked up a bucket of kitchen scraps by the back door. "Here, Mac, come out to the barn; there's something you've got to see." She led the way out into the yard and through a side door into her poultry barn. "It's been a weird day, I can tell you that much! Careful, stay back a bit—they can be nasty."

"Who?"

"My Chinese geese," she replied, pointing at a flock of large white birds on the other side of the barn. "Would you believe it—all six of them were laying this morning! I'm not sure what's gotten into them—usually they don't lay at all this time of year, but today, the whole gaggle!"

The big white birds waddled towards us, the orange hump over top of their bills making them look just a bit menacing as they honked at us. I took a picture of them anyway.

"Oh shoo!" Mary-Lou said to the geese. "Don't bite the hand that feeds you, you silly things." She put the scraps into the feeding trough the birds all shared, and while they were busy rooting through their treats, she ran her hand under some straw in the corner of the room. "Gotcha!" She drew out a large egg, almost as big as her hand. "There, that was the last one; I think I've got them all now. I don't want the ducks sitting on them yet; it's far too cold for raising goslings this time of year."

As we walked back to Mary-Lou's house, I absentmindedly thumbed through the photos on my phone. The geese—all six of them. The five rings at Engelhard's. Four birds at Lilian's feeder, calling to each other. Mary-Lou's three French hens. Lilian's two mourning doves, which she called turtle doves. And there, in my parents' backyard, the partridge in the pear tree.

"Mary-Lou…" I held out the phone to her.

"What?" She took the phone and looked at it. "You already showed me that; it's the text from Tom that we can't figure out."

I snatched back the phone. "Wait—no, that's not what I meant to show you, my finger must have slipped. But..." I stared down at the text. "Twelve Days of Christmas? The whole thing? Mary-Lou—he means the *song*. There's something about that song. And I've seen it—every single day since Christmas Day. One item every day. So where is he? What the heck is going on?"

THE SEVENTH DAY OF CHRISTMAS

My work day had never seemed as long as it did on that New Year's Eve. I snapped at old Ernie Smith when he took so long to decide which antacid he wanted, the 10 or the 20 mg, and had to apologize; and then had to apologize again when I sent a mom with two sneezing, snotty-nosed, whining kids down the wrong aisle in pursuit of cold medicine. Finally, when I realized I had counted out the one hundred tablets of Malvinia Shoemaker's heart medication in the double-strength dose instead of the single-strength, I threw in the towel.

"Look, Gina," I said to the pharmacist, "I think I need to call it a day. I can't think straight; you'll have to double-check everything I've done in the last hour or two. I'm really sorry. Do you mind if I knock off early? I don't want to accidentally poison anyone."

Gina looked over the top of her reading glasses down the empty aisles of the drug store. "Go ahead, I think I can hold down the fort. Are you all right?"

"Yeah, yeah, pretty much. Just—well, you know."

She gave me a sympathetic look. "It'll be fine," she said soothingly. "He'll turn up."

"I hope so," I said and rubbed my aching temple.

Gina raised an eyebrow. "You're not coming down with something, are you?"

I gave a humourless laugh. "I'm not sure." Was a case of "The Twelve Days of Christmas" a diagnosable condition?

"Well, better get some rest, then. Give the New Year's Eve parties a miss."

"Hadn't planned on going to one, anyway, even if..." I'd wanted to just spend it with Tom, watch the TV broadcast, toast with a glass of champagne... "Thanks, Gina. I'll see you Wednesday." I hung my white lab coat on the hook behind the door of the staff room and headed out to my car.

As I put the key in the lock, suddenly there was a hand on my arm. I turned my head and looked into Celia Whitewell's wrinkle-framed brown eyes, her grey hair hanging wildly around her face.

"This is the year," she said urgently. "Right around now, that's when they took him. And every twelve years, the portal opens again; that's when they come back through. I didn't manage to get to him last time, or the time before, but now, but now... In the twelve days, every twelve years..."

And a hey nonny nonny, I'm sure. Poor

20

woman.

I soothingly patted Celia's hand, then gently removed her clutch from my sleeve. But she wasn't even paying attention to me anymore.

"Every twelve years…" she muttered, and she shuffled away towards the big grey structure of the community hall which was probably as old as she was.

Where to now? I had called everyone I could think of to ask about Tom, but no luck. However, I still had not gone out to Carson's Landing to track down that lady. Why had I been procrastinating on this so long? It was almost like I was scared to go out there. But the last person I knew had seen Tom before he disappeared was there. I had to do this.

Resolutely I turned the key in the ignition, shifted the car into gear and pulled out of the parking lot.

Ten minutes later, I turned down the side road off the highway that led to Carson's Landing. Old Jimbo Carson had lived right at the very end of it, in a small house—more of a cottage, really—that his grandfather had built there in the days of the gold rush.

The building that stood on the site of Jimbo's little house now was certainly no cottage—I hardly even wanted to call it a house. "Mansion" was more like it, if not "palace"—a very modern one, at least. Three stories tall, it had two floors of wrap-around decks with Plexiglas railings facing the lake, and the roof on the lake side came to a high peak in the centre, with glass, glass and more glass instead of walls.

I parked the car and turned off the ignition, sitting there and staring at the place. It didn't look like anyone was home inside that glass castle—was there? They were probably out doing New Year's Eve somewhere. Maybe I should just leave again.

But no! I'd never find Tom if I was chicken. Tom… I gave myself a mental kick in the pants and got out of the car. Suddenly lights flared up inside the building and over the front door, their brightness making me realize that dusk was not far away.

The door opened and a figure stood outlined against the inside lights.

"Hello! Can I help you with anything?" a beautiful baritone called out to me.

Mr. Jewellery Store Guy! Once again I got that strange fluttering in my stomach and a strong sense of vertigo.

"Umm, uh—" Get a grip, Mac! I gave myself a push away from the car and forced my wobbly knees to walk in the direction of the house. "I'm, uh, looking for someone. Uh, my, my…"

"Yes?" He flashed me that thousand-watt smile, and again it seemed to knock the stuffing out of me.

"It's, uh, um… Actually, I'm looking for Tom," I said. "My, uh—he's a friend. And someone said that—" I was making no sense, and he was still beaming that smile at me. "N-never mind," I stammered. I was obviously at the wrong place, wasn't I? "I think I'll just, uh, go."

"Yes, maybe you should," the man said, but the waves of charm that radiated off him made it seem as if he had just issued the most cordial invitation to come into the house.

"Y-yes," I said, taking a step closer, "maybe…"

"Who is it, Galaeron?" a melodious woman's voice came from inside the house. I had never heard such an attractive voice before—well, not before I had heard the man's. This was a woman's version of the same honeyed, dulcet tones that made me want to sink into whatever it was they were offering, made me want to stay and never leave… I took one more step towards the house.

A woman's face appeared over the man's shoulder. White-blonde hair flowed back in ripples from a smooth white forehead; silver-grey eyes that were set at a slant looked at me from under incongruously dark, perfectly straight eyebrows; and a tiny mouth with delicately rosy lips formed into a pout.

"Well?" she said, raising one of her perfect eyebrows.

In her own way, she was as stunning as the man, but I couldn't stand her—which was what saved me. The antipathy I felt slapped my brain back to functionality.

"I'm looking for my b- my friend Tom," I said. "About your height—" I gestured at the man, "dark hair, brown eyes. Someone said they saw you," I looked at the woman, "talking to him on Christmas Eve, and nobody has seen him since."

She gave an affected laugh, as silvery and metallic as her eyes. "Am I supposed to have done away with him? I'm sorry, I can't help you. I don't even remember talking to this—Tom." She laid her left hand caressingly on the man's shoulder, as if to say she had no need for the likes of Tom—and what I saw then snapped me out of the last of my daze. On her left ring finger sparkled the princess-cut diamond from Engelhard's.

"All right," I said, and I heard a slight hiss in my voice. "I just thought I'd ask. Goodbye."

I turned to leave, and there on the lake shore

beside the house I saw them: seven perfect white swans, swimming in one line along the encroaching ice of the shoreline. I pulled out my phone, shook it to open the camera, and clicked the shutter.

When I turned back to the house, the door was closed and the lights inside had gone dark.

THE EIGHTH DAY OF CHRISTMAS

I was out early again on New Year's Day. The streets in town were dead—all the stores were closed, of course, and not even Dinah's Diner had the "Open" sign out. But I didn't need any of them, anyway; I was headed out of town.

Right at midnight, while I had been sniffling into my lonesome glass of champagne in front of the TV that showed the ball dropping in Times Square, the penny dropped in my mind. For all of last week, I had been waiting for something to turn up, had been half angry with Tom for vanishing as he did, had figured the police would find him. But as the crowd in Times Square in their backwards count to midnight reached zero, it had burst on me with more explosions and sparks than the fireworks: I had to get Tom back. Filing the missing persons report with the police wouldn't do it—I had to go myself.

I knew it was something to do with that mansion at Carson's Landing, and the two gorgeous people who had denied seeing him. With that woman who wore the ring that Joe Engelhard had hinted had been bought by Tom. So I was going back out there, and I was going to look, and knock, and ask questions, until I found *something*.

But I drew another blank. The fancy house was, this time, actually empty. No answer to my knocking and doorbell-ringing, no response to my wandering around the outside, tapping on windows, and even trying to peer in through the glass. Nobody home. Not even the swans were in sight on the lakeshore.

I got back in my car and stared out the window at the lake. Across the inlet, I could see the big barn of Whitewell's Dairy Farm, where Celia still lived with her brother's family. They were the nearest neighbours to the Carson place—maybe they knew where the inhabitants of the lakeshore palace had gone off to.

Fifteen minutes later, I pulled up in front of the Whitewell's big barn. The door stood half open, and I could hear voices and the sound of machinery. I supposed that even on New Year's Day the animals had to be taken care of on their regular schedule. I got out of the car and stuck my head into the barn. The warm smell of milk and cattle dung met my nose; black-and-white cow rumps lined up side by side to the right and left of the central walkway, stretching what seemed like a long ways into the distance. There was a rhythmic hissing noise, like some pneumatic machinery, and gently the tails of the cows swished back and forth as if keeping time to it.

Down the central aisle of the barn, a young girl and a guy walked towards me, carrying a piece of shiny machinery with hoses hanging off it. Oh, no, the second person was a girl, too—the short hair and baseball cap had me confused for a moment.

She looked at me with her eyebrows raised. "Hey, anything we can do for you?"

"Hi," I said, "sorry to bug you while you're working—"

"It's okay," she said, "we're always working. Life of the dairy farmer. The milking has to be done, no matter what."

"I guess. Well, I was just wondering. I'm looking for someone—my friend Tom. I'm asking around if anyone's seen him."

Another short-cropped girl's head poked around the rear end of a cow just a few stalls down from where I stood.

"Do you mean Tom Rimer?" the girl asked. "Tallish, dark, drives a black 1970 Chevy pickup with purple fenders?"

"Yes!!" I said. "Yes! Have you seen him? Was he here?"

The girl shrugged. "Sorry, haven't seen him—but his truck's been parked by the forest road, just the other side of our property line, for about a week. At least I think it's his truck."

Of course it was Tom's truck; it was the only one of its kind in town. It had been in almost mint condition when he bought it a couple years back; it used to belong to Eldon, the guy that disappeared back in '71, and it had sat in storage ever since. Finally, a sign of Tom's whereabouts!

"Oh!" A fourth girl came out from between two cows further down the barn. "Is that whose truck that is? Do you know if he'd consider selling?"

"Em, you need another truck like you need a hole in the head!" the first girl said.

The Em girl pouted. "But I want it, it's really cute!"

She sounded like a grade school kid with her Barbie doll collection. Now I remembered: the Whitewells had a whole lot of daughters. Four, or five—yes, there was another one, way down the other end of the barn. Oh, six! Yet another one. That was a lot of girls. As far as I knew, they were all adults, and most of them lived away; they must have come home for a holiday visit.

"So, Tom's truck is here?" I said, excitement making me feel tingly all over. "Do you have any idea where he went from here?"

The first girl shook her head. "Not me," she said. "Em? Mara? Cally?" The three girls that were closest to my end of the barn shook their heads. "So, sorry, can't help you," she said. "If you want to stick around until we're done the milking, might be able to talk it over then and see what we can do." She hoisted her shiny machine and turned to the nearest cow rump.

At the far end of the barn, I could see yet another two figures emerging from between the cattle, and they and the last two that had come out looked like they were staring at me. I gave myself a slight shake. Eight girls. Eight girls in a barn, milking the cows.

Surreptitiously, I took out my phone, booted up the camera, and took a picture of the length of the barn.

The girl farthest down the building was waving

at me—beckoning me. Did she want to tell me something? Those four at the other end of the barn hadn't responded to the first girl's question. Suddenly I knew, without a shadow of a doubt, that they knew something. Something about Tom.

I hitched my purse higher on my shoulder and walked down the long aisle of the barn over the squeaky-clean polished cement. Somewhere half-way down, my foot caught on something—for a split second, it felt as if I had walked into an invisible wall.

But I kept going, walking towards the four girls at the far end of the barn. They just stood there. So did their cows—where the ones at the front of the barn vigorously swished their tails and rustled around in their stalls, these ones held perfectly still. In fact, they looked fake, as if they were nothing but movie props—cardboard cutouts.

I looked at the girls as I got closer. They looked familiar. Really familiar. They looked—they looked just like the other four girls in the front section of the barn. Two of them with short blonde hair, one with medium-length brown hair, one with a ponytail under a backwards baseball cap; all of them wearing jeans or overalls and rubber boots. I looked back towards the front section of the barn, and then ahead to the back section. The one was a mirror image of the other.

"What's going on here?" I could hear slight hysteria in my voice.

"Nothing," said the girl who was the double of the first girl. "You want to find Tom? We can help you."

They were giving me the creeps, with their silent, unwavering smiles and the motionless cows between them. Yes, I needed to find Tom, but not with *their* help!

"No thanks!" I said. "I'll be leaving now, thank you!"

With a few strides, I reached the barn door and pulled it open.

In front of me was a spring meadow in full bloom.

THE NINTH DAY OF CHRISTMAS

I stepped through the door of the barn out into the meadow. Birds were singing; flowers were blooming all around—daisies, buttercups, Indian paintbrush, black-eyed Susans, you name it. There were even blinkin' *butterflies* fluttering over it all. All that was missing was a frolicking little baah-lamb. Baah, Humbug!

This was baloney. I looked around, trying to orient myself. Would I be able to get back? The barn door behind me was still there, except from this angle the building looked like a romantically decayed hay shed, overgrown with picturesque ivy. Whatever—so long as I could get back out through it.

Turning around, I saw that the hyper-beautiful meadow in one direction extended to the edge of a supernaturally green forest, in the other rose up to the brow of a gentle hill. I couldn't see any point in going into the forest—who knew what lurked there; I didn't trust all this unreal and unseasonal beauty. I set out in the other direction and crested the brow of the little hill. Beyond that the meadow was curving away down a hillside, a path leading down into a lush green valley.

I had only walked for a few hundred metres when around a bend in the path I came on another green field. This one was not a picturesque alpine meadow strewn with wildflowers, but an equally picturesque groomed lawn, velvety-smooth and emerald green. It was surrounded by a low hedge spilling over with rose blossoms; a tent pavilion stood in its centre, gleaming white in the sunshine, with pennants in every colour of the rainbow glittering from its pinnacle. Beautiful people gently strolled about in front of it, the hems of the ladies' gowns gliding over the grass, the men bending their shapely heads to hear what their companions were saying. I could hear strains of enticing music, and I was overcome with an urge to go over to find out what was creating this unearthly beautiful sound. I had to hear more of it, had to be near it, experience it, be among those beautiful people, be one of them. Walking on a little ways along the rose hedge, I came to a small opening, a gate just wide enough to let me in—as if it had been meant for me.

I stepped through, and was about to hurry towards the pavilion, when my eye fell on a person. A male person, apparently, dark-haired and dressed in dark blue pants and a grey shirt, sitting on the ground beside a little bush to the side of the path. He intently gazed at a little square flat thing in his hands, not longer than the palm of his hand, and periodically stabbed at it with his finger.

I frowned. There was something familiar about him. Where did I know him from? Something stirred in my memory. Wasn't this the man I had met just recently—the most beautiful man I had ever seen? The man for whose sake I had come to this place, to be with him forever?

I gazed at him, willing him to lift his head, so I could see his mesmerizing silver-grey eyes, could exchange with him the loving glance that was sure to follow when he caught sight of me.

His fingers fumbled, and the square thing dropped from his hand and landed on his foot.

He flinched, snatched the thing up from the ground, and looked up.

His eyes met mine. Not silver-grey, but brown.

We stared at each other for what seemed like an eternity.

All of a sudden, it was as if someone had turned a fan on the woolly fog that had filled my brain, and I could see in his eyes that it happened to him at the same time. Tom!

We rushed towards each other, but then Tom froze, throwing out his hands in a gesture that stopped me in my tracks. I opened my mouth to speak, but he frantically shook his head, pressing his fingers to his lips to tell me to be silent. He pointed to his left, and I turned my head to look.

From out of the green trees on the edge of the meadow came a procession of the most beautiful ladies I had ever seen. Stately and lithe, grave and merry, clear and mysterious all at once, they twirled and glided over the meadow, their motion in perfect harmony with the strains of the unearthly music that came from the white silk pavilion. A dance of ethereal beauty, performed by the most perfect physical beings I had ever laid eyes on. Nine of these ladies there were, led by one whose white-gold hair floated past her waist, setting off the silvery blue of her gown.

But wait—I had seen her before! I knew this not with the woolly-headed vagueness that had afflicted me when I first caught sight of Tom, but with a razor-sharp clarity that allowed for no mistake. This was the woman that had been in the house on Carson's Landing—the one who wore the ring that *I* had been hoping for.

I turned to look at Tom to tell him what I knew, but I saw him staring at the lady, mesmerized. He moved slowly, as if he was in a trance—and then I noticed what he was doing: he was trying to lift the cell phone he was still clutching in his fingers, but his arm moved as if he was dragging it through molasses.

Nine ladies dancing!

I whipped out my own phone, shook the camera open, held it out and pressed the volume button. The shutter clicked—and with the sound, Tom came out of his trance.

His head flew around and he stared at me, then he pulled me down to the ground beside the little bush, out of sight of the dancing ladies.

I drew breath to protest, but he clapped his hand over my mouth.

"Don't!" he mouthed soundlessly. "Do not speak!"

I nodded just slightly, and he took his hand from my face. Then he mimed zipping shut his lips.

"Oh-kay," I formed with my lips, nodding and

copying his zip-the-lip gesture for good measure.

He gave a quick nod of approval, then his head came up and he froze.

I cautiously sat up and looked over the bush. There, not ten metres away with his back to us, stood the gorgeous man from Engelhard's.

My eyes widened. Him! The most wonderful man in the world! He was the one I had come here for! My one true love, my—

Something painfully flicked me on the ear. I hissed in a breath, and the pink cotton candy cloud disappeared from my brain. Tom was holding his thumb over the nail of his middle finger, poised to give me another flick on the ear, but at the sight of the glare I directed at him he hurriedly lowered his hand and changed it into a thumbs-up gesture.

I grinned. Then I pointed with my thumb over my shoulder at the people in the middle of the meadow, towards whom the not-really-all-that-gorgeous guy was strolling now. "What are they?" I mouthed at Tom.

He responded the same way. "Elves."

I frowned at him incredulously, and he nodded.

"E-L-V-E-S," he spelled out laboriously in finger alphabet.

"Really?" I mouthed.

He nodded, then he raised his finger in an expression of "I just had an idea." He took his cell phone and pulled up the notepad program.

"*Lured me in,*" he typed. "*Can't talk out loud, else stuck. Elvis said.*"

That had to be a typo; he probably meant "elves". And why would they tell him that?

Tom saw the expression on my face, and he

35

shook his head.

"No no no!" he mouthed. "Not elves—El*vis*!"

He pointed at the name on the phone screen and then into the crowd around the pavilion, and all of a sudden it was perfectly obvious what he meant. I was surprised I hadn't noticed the man before, he was so different from the ethereal creatures he was standing among. Although he was tall and dark like several of them, he was dressed head to toe in a white jumpsuit with pinwheel patterns made of rivets all over it, holding a snare drum under his arm as if he was in the middle of setting up the stage for a concert. But most importantly, in spite of his outfit, of his enormous sideburns, and of the ostentatious black curl that dipped into his forehead, even in spite of the dreamy expression on his face as he stared at the elven lady who was now gliding into the pavilion, somehow he looked real.

He *was* real, even if he had not aged a day in forty-eight years. Celia had been right all along.

Tom tugged my sleeve and held out the phone, showing me the message. "*What day is it?*"

I grabbed the phone from his hand.

"*Jan 1,*" I typed.

His eyebrows climbed to his forehead and he took the phone back.

"*Took me @ xmas eve,*" he typed. "*Thought it was only xmas day. U sure it's Jan 1?*"

I shrugged. If this place warped time perception so much that he hadn't felt eight days go by, it could be just about any date now.

Tom's thumbs were flying over the keyboard.

"*12 days of xmas song will get us out,*" he typed, "*Elvis said.*"

I nodded vigorously. I'd known that! I quickly pulled out my phone, booted up the picture gallery and tabbed through the pictures, starting with the partridge in the pear tree.

Tom's eyes widened. "Yes!" he mouthed, excitedly jabbing his thumbs up into the air.

But when I got to the picture of the eight girls in the barn—or the eight maids a-milking, as it were— my jaw dropped. There was the barn, and the rumps of the cows, and the four girls I had talked to at first— but in the back half of the barn, which wasn't nearly as big as it had appeared, there were only a few empty cattle stalls, and scattered among them, four weird things. Splotches of light overlaid with shapes that looked like something Dr. Seuss might have drawn while on drugs. Eew, not attractive.

I quickly swiped the picture to the right—and sure enough, the nine ladies dancing over the meadow were just the same: weird creatures laid over light splotches. The background showed as a stark, empty field, with a few bare trees and not much else. I shivered, and Tom put his arm around me, rubbing my shoulder. He looked down at my phone and gave me a questioning look.

I nodded. Yes, those had been the dancing ladies. But hang on—if it was the nine ladies dancing, it had to be the ninth day! I pointed at Tom's cell phone where I had typed "Jan 1", shook my head and made a "two" gesture with my fingers.

Tom frowned.

"*Time moving too fast,*" he typed, "*u gotta get out of here or they get u 2.*"

I stared at him. I wasn't leaving without him!

He shook his head.

"Can't leave til you get all 12 days," he typed and pointed at my phone.

Get them all? How on Earth was I supposed to pull that off?

Tom took me by the shoulders, turned me around and gave me a gentle shove.

"Go," he mouthed at me, "please!"

He tapped his wrist where his watch would be, if he ever wore one, and twirled his forefinger in a "hurry up" gesture. Time was passing!

A shot of fear skittered down my spine. What if it was already too late? What if the last few days had already come and gone while we were stuck here talking, and I had missed the mark?

THE TENTH DAY OF CHRISTMAS

I stumbled through the door of the fake hay shed and emerged into cold darkness. Slowly my eyes adjusted, and I blinked. Not only had I gone from a bright spring day back into a winter night, this wasn't even the inside of the Whitewell's dairy barn. I stood in the alley behind the community hall in town, having apparently just stepped out of the back door of the second-hand bookstore next to it. The yellow lamp over the doorway lit up the softly drifting snowfall, and now I became aware of the traffic noises from Main Street on the other side of the hall. Not too late in the night then—this town rolls up its sidewalks by 10:00 PM; nobody is out and about past that hour.

As if to prove my point, a vehicle turned in at the end of the alley and came racing towards me—well, maybe not racing, but still moving rather more quickly than is advisable in a dark, snowy back alley. I flattened myself against the hall's brick wall and gave the driver the stink-eye as he skidded to a halt on the other side of the hall door. He choked off the engine and leaped from the truck, and now I recognized him: it was Marty Wardle, a coworker of Tom's. It looked like he had just come off his work shift, his hard hat and lamp still on his head and his face smeared with coal dust.

"Hey Mac," he tossed over his shoulder as he stabbed the code into the security panel, yanked open the hall door and vanished inside. The door spilled a rush of light, warmth and sound into the darkness. I could make out the sound of a fiddle and drums, and over it all the rhythmic jingling of bells and a strange clacking noise, punctuated by shouts. The door slowly swung shut, but I jumped and grabbed the handle before it closed all the way and left me out in the cold. The stale-coffee-and-industrial-dishwasher smell of the hall's back corridor assaulted my nostrils just as the music broke off abruptly. I side-stepped into the kitchen, walked around its middle island with the cracked purple arborite countertop worn from decades of community events, and peered through the serving hutch into the hall.

A group of men stood in a circle in the middle, all of them dressed just like Marty in hard hats, dirty work overalls and steel-toed boots, their faces sooty with coal dust.

"About time you got here, man," one of them called out to Marty, who had just joined the group.

Marty shrugged. "Sorry, had to go back and double-check Valve Six."

There were a few grunts of approval around

40

the circle as Marty reached for a can of beer from a flat on a side table that also held a large silver boom box. I recognized most of these men—Lord's Mine employees, all of them, as far as I could make out. It was a little hard to tell under all the soot.

"Well, you're here now, let's get on with it," said a stocky guy whose bib overall strained over a belly that has been the final resting place for at least two fried chickens and a case of Molson Canadian per week for as long as I've known him. Foreman Herb Downing has no need for artificial padding when he plays Santa Claus for the local elementary school every December.

He stepped over to the boombox, hit a button, and the Celtic fiddle and drums started up again.

"Where's my stick?" Marty shouted over the music, tossing back the last of his beer and crushing the can in his fist, then chucking it at the blue recycling bin under the table.

Herb gestured into the corner with his own stick, a thick three-foot-long staff of plain wood.

"A-one-and-two-and-" he counted out, his foot stomping the rhythm, setting the bells tied around his ankle jingling.

Marty snatched up his stick and fell into step in the circle.

Stomp, step, stomp, jump—they struck their staffs together, leapt back out of the circle and back in, stomp, step, and a-clack and a-jingle, stomp, step, shout—the Lord's Mine Morris Men in action, practising for the Twelfth Night parade on Sunday. It was a sight to behold, and as always, I couldn't help but tap my foot and beat the rhythm of their dance against my thigh.

Tom was supposed to be one of them—why

41

hadn't they missed him? At the very least, they should be one man short in the routine! But the pattern didn't look unbalanced. I started counting the spinning bodies. Two, four, five—Marty, Herb… I lost track and had to start over again. How many were there meant to be? It definitely wasn't the usual six or sets of four—I knew that when the original owner of Lord's Mine had brought the tradition over from his native England, he couldn't find the right number of dancers, so they made up their own to go with their idiosyncratic "costume" of just wearing their work clothes with the addition of bells and staffs.

"Whoa!" Herb yelled as the swing of his partner's staff went wide and glanced off the burly foreman's hard hat, knocking it askew. "Watch it there, buster!"

The whirling dancer spun away from him with a stomp of his boot, his bells jingling, a smile on his face. It served Herb right; it was probably his own fault he'd been hit in the head. It couldn't be this elegant, graceful man's fault; he was easily the best dancer in the lot. I didn't even begrudge him having taken Tom's place in the figures.

Two, four, six, Herb, the beautiful dancer—and I'd lost track again, staring at this man. Who *was* he? I didn't recognize him under the blackface. And he *was* wearing blackface, not just the coal dust layer that the others had on, left over from their work shifts. Full, smeared-on blackface. Didn't he know that wasn't acceptable anymore? None of the others were made up that heavily. I looked around the circle of dancers and subconsciously kept counting.

Six, seven—a leap and a stomp, a step and a clack—eight, nine—a stomp and a shout, a leap and—

ten! There were ten of them! Ten Lord's men leaping!

As I whipped out my phone, shook it open and clicked the shutter button, the recognition fell into place: the blackface who had usurped Tom's place was the seductive elf lord. And just as the shock of the realization ran down my spine like in an icy trickle, he looked up and his silver eyes locked with mine.

There was no more sweet, seductive allure in that glance. It had become a dagger-sharp threat.

THE ELEVENTH DAY OF CHRISTMAS

The door at the front of the hall swung open, and in trooped the remaining workers of Lord's late shift.

"About time," Herb greeted them as the Morris dancers stopped their whirl. "Did you bring the tin whistles?"

The big bearded guy at the front of the line hoisted a pink tote bag, its delicate colour incongruous against the coal dust that was permanently ground into the skin of his beefy hands. "That's why we were late. I couldn't find them; my damn girlfriend packed them all into here."

"And of course, he couldn't touch that bag to check inside it," one of the others said with a smirk, "it might have made him look more girly than he already

44

is."

A ribald chorus of laughter greeted this sally, and as the tote bag carrier put his burden on the table perhaps a little less gently than he could have I could hear the metallic sound of pipes clattering together.

"All right, let's do this thing," said Herb. "Who's got the music?"

Marty pulled a sheaf of papers out from underneath the boombox. "You do, genius."

"Well, yeah, uh," Herb spluttered. Then he tugged on the straps of his overall bib and squared his shoulders. "Of course I do." He twitched the papers out of Marty's hand and started handing them out, seemingly at random.

"I'm not playing," Marty said, his hands raised in protest as Herb shoved a paper at him. "I'm tone deaf, remember?"

"So will the rest of us be after this," said the tote bag guy. "I don't know whose damn idea this was in the first place." It looked like he still hadn't gotten over the teasing about the pink bag.

"It's traditional," said Herb firmly, plunging his hand into the offending bag and coming out with a bouquet of gleaming metal tubes with bright-coloured plastic whistle heads. "Or at least it will be after this year."

The big guy made a huffing noise, but he pulled a scarlet-headed tin whistle out of Herb's hands like he was drawing a straw. The little instrument nearly disappeared in his huge hand.

"I still think it's stupid," he said.

"Then why'd you order the things from Amazon?" one of the other fellows said. "You were all for it when Herb brought it up the other day."

"Because he used to play one in marching band back in high school," Marty said, "and he was damn good at it too, even I could tell. Herb, do you still need the rest of us, or are we through here with the dance?"

Herb threw a cursory glance around the hall. "If you could stick around for a bit, let's run through the Morris again after this," he said. "We could use a bit more practice."

"All right." Marty grabbed another can of beer from the table and leaned against the wall next to two other soot-covered miners.

Marty was right—the big guy was good. As soon as he put the little flute to his lips, his bad mood seemed to drop off him. His eyes lit up, and a lilting, dancing stream of notes flowed from the whistle. He never even glanced at the sheet of music lying on the table in front of him.

Herb looked at him with his jaw dropped. "Shit, man!" he said when the big guy's tune stopped. "Why'd you never tell me about this before?"

The guy shrugged, looking embarrassed. "Didn't think of it," he mumbled.

Herb raised his eyebrows, then turned to the others. "Okay! Any other closet James Galways in you lot?"

"James Galways?" one of the other guys asked, tossing back another beer.

"Forget it," Herb said. "Who can play one of these things?" He held out the bundle of whistles with their coloured plastic heads.

I counted. It would have been too much to ask for there to be eleven—wouldn't it? Two orange, three green, three blue and two black. Ten. My shoulders slumped.

"Come on," Herb said, shaking the whistles at the miners. The guys looked at each other, then after some shrugging, embarrassed looks, and shoving each other forward—"You do it!" "No, you do it!"—enough of them stepped up to form the whistle band.

The big guy hadn't been kidding with his quip about going deaf—the squeaky racket most of them produced from the whistles was painful. He winced.

"C'mon, guys!" he yelled over the noise. "This isn't rocket science!" He waved his scarlet-headed tin whistle at them.

Scarlet? Wait—I had forgotten to count his whistle in the total! My heart suddenly hammered in my ears so hard the sound drowned out the shrieks of the tortured tin whistles. There were eleven! Eleven pipes, and eleven pipers!

Could you call the noise they were making "piping"? Did it count if it wasn't actual music? I took out my phone, but my hands trembled so much I couldn't open the camera.

"*Shut up*!!" the big guy yelled over the din. About half of the guys listened and took their whistles from their mouths, but three or four of them, who had been making serious inroads into the beer before consenting to try the whistles, had now gotten into a contest as to who could produce the most hideous screeching noise from their instrument, and they fell about laughing, shoving each other back and forth between taking blasts on their pipes, crashing into the people standing next to and behind them. One of those was the blackface elf lord, but he seemed completely unfazed by the jolt. In fact, he was staring at the rambunctious miners with a most peculiar look on his face—was he actually egging them on, somehow?

And why was the hall so crowded all of a sudden—where had all those extra people come from?

"SHUT! UP!" tin whistle guy roared, and when that had no effect, he tore the whistle from the lips of the fellow next to him who was producing a particularly earsplitting shriek, and he smashed it over his skull. The crack of the instrument's plastic head splitting reverberated right through my bones.

No!! Not the eleventh pipe!

I must have cried out, because several of the faces in the hall turned towards me and stared.

And among the stares were the triumphant-looking silver eyes of not only the elf lord, but also the lady.

In fact, I noticed through the haze of my disappointment, the extra crowd in the hall was made up of the beautiful elf people, more of them drifting in ethereally through the open door at the back. Their deadly beauty seemed incongruous among the coal-faced miners, who had been shocked into acquiescence by the big guy's outburst and were now at least attempting to generate something akin to music with their pipes. Not that it mattered anymore, as there were only ten pipes left, and the elves knew it and were gloating over it.

I slumped to the ground against the kitchen island and buried my head in my arms. A tremendous fatigue washed over me. Was there any hope left to help Tom? True, it was only the tenth day; not time for the pipers anyway… I pulled out my phone to check the time. 11:59 PM. As I looked, the time clicked over to midnight: the eleventh day had begun.

Slowly it penetrated my consciousness that the

sound coming from the other side of the serving hatch between the kitchen and the hall was no longer horrific screeching noises—it was music. Lilting, beautiful tunes, like a Celtic dance. I grabbed the edge of the counter, pulled myself up and looked through the serving hatch into the hall.

What I saw surprised a laugh out of me in spite of myself. The burly miners in their sooty overalls and clunky workboots were dancing—dancing in a gentle shuffle, swaying to the tune of their own melodious piping, a transcendent look on their scruffy faces. Behind them, on the other side of their circle, stood the elf lord, his face miraculously no longer black-smeared, conducting their dance with a wave of his slender white hands, a malicious gleam in his eyes.

His waving hands took on a pulsing rhythm, and the miners became a marching pipe band. A-one-two-three, they marched up the hall, turned a right angle at the end, turned again and marched back towards me; another sharp right, ten steps along the short side of the hall—they walked by me right in front of the serving hutch, their eyes glazed with the spell they were under. My fingers twitched to reach through and grab their sleeves, shake them out of their trance, but I knew it was pointless. They swept past me, turned the corner and marched back up the hall to the tune of their own piping.

The elf lord's face wore an expression of wicked exultation, and the lady and the other elves beside him clapped their hands in a gleeful rhythm, marking time with the marching players.

But suddenly there was another movement in the corner of the hall that went counter to the swaying movement. A shadowy form that looked different from the elves, not ethereally beautiful, but stocky and dark-haired, was weaving its way through the crowd.

Tom! He had made it out, he was here! My heart did a jump in my chest. We had won, he was free!

But—no. There was something wrong. He looked ... he looked off. Wrong-coloured, somehow, as if there was weird lighting on him. Yes, that was it—the light that fell on his head and shoulders looked like sunlight on a spring day, not the blue flickering of the fluorescent tubes that lit up the hall. He wasn't really here—or was he?

And *what* was he doing?

The marching band of piping miners had reached the far end of the hall again, the elf lord made them do another right turn, and they strode back towards me, skirling all the while. Suddenly Tom ducked around the backs of two elegantly swaying elves. With three more strides he reached the back of the marching line and fell into step with his piping workmates. Was he caught in the spell as well? No, please no...

Then he raised his two hands, cupped them together to form a ball, put them to his lips, and blew into them through his thumbs. Right over the tune of the pipers I could hear the hooting note of his dove call.

Tom himself was being the eleventh piper!

I whipped up my phone and clicked the shutter button.

Suddenly the scene froze. The piping miners stopped dead in their tracks, several of them with their feet half-raised in mid-stride, and the big guy at the head of the line had his eyes closed, obviously caught right as he was blinking.

The elves turned their head and stared at Tom, their silver-eyed glare like icicles.

"What is this?" the elf lady cried out, her gown swirling up around her as if she was generating a furious wind. "How dare he!"

"We will deal with him," the elf lord said, and at his imperious hand gesture two of the elves jumped forward and grabbed Tom, their sharp nails digging into his arms. "Take him!" the elf lord cried, and the room became a stream of motion as they dragged Tom backwards, past the immobile miners, and he was taken with them as they flowed out the door.

But as he was borne out between the steel door posts, he turned his head, and he gave me a wink.

THE TWELFTH DAY OF CHRISTMAS

I sprang forward just as the hall door was beginning to close after the last elf had wafted through the opening. I got my foot in the crack, then pushed outward against the heavy steel panel. I was *not* letting them take Tom from me again. And if I could not free him, then they would have to keep me as well.

Leaving behind me the sound of the confused muttering of the miners waking from their trance, I stepped through the door. As I had half expected, I arrived not in the darkness of the back alley behind the hall, but in the brilliant sunshine of the fake elven spring. I rubbed my eyes, dazzled by the sudden change in light, and it took me a minute to realize where I was.

I stood among the trees at the edge of the supernaturally green meadow, looking at the gleaming white tent pavilion in the middle, where the elf lady sat enthroned on jewel-toned silk cushions. The elf lord stood beside her, and they gazed with disdain at Tom, who was being helplessly dragged towards them, then thrown on his knees before them.

"You think you can win your way back to your world by trickery?" the lady said, her voice like ice shards. "Do not fool yourself, mortal!"

I could barely stand to look at Tom. He knelt at the lady's feet, his head bowed, his shoulders slumped. Defeated, he raised his hands, clutching at hers, begging for mercy. Silently. He would not speak— could not speak—please, Tom, do not speak!

"He is not worth your time," the elf lord said contemptuously, clamping his hand on Tom's shoulder and yanking him back from her. "Take him away. Guards!"

Immediately, a loud thrumming sound began in the forest behind me.

Tum-tu-rum, tum-tada-rum, tum-tum-tum…

In two rows, one from my right, one from my left, they stepped out from between the trees. Two lines of drummers, dressed in guards' uniforms, like giant stereotypical nutcrackers. *Rum-tada-tum, rum-ta-dum*— step by step they advanced into the meadow, converging on where Tom was cowering before the icy elf woman.

Drummers!

I raised my phone, ready to shoot. This was it! One more picture, and we had them all.

But there, what was this? My eye scanned down the line of the red-coated nutcracker elves. Two, four, six—wait! Eight, ten. They had done it again. There were only ten.

Out of the corner of my eye I saw a motion. A white figure sauntered out from the crowd milling about the meadow, the pinwheel pattern of the rivets on his Elvis suit sparkling. He carried his snare drum under his arm, and he wandered over, falling into step behind the last nutcracker, sleepily tapping on the drum head with his fingers.

Oh! Thank you, Elvis! Now there were … there still weren't enough. There were only eleven.

In despair, I looked over at Tom. The elf lord had an iron hand on his shoulder, holding him down on his knees. There was no way Tom could pull off the same trick twice, and the elves knew it, too. A wickedly triumphant look travelled between the elf lord and the lady, and she looked down with a sneer at Tom.

That did it.

I was not going to let those bastards win. Twelve drummers we needed in the picture, and twelve drummers we were going to have.

Right at that moment, Elvis turned his head, and with eyes that were anything but sleepy looked straight at me.

But I didn't need him to tell me.

In one motion, I jumped to my feet, whirled around with my back to the scene in the meadow, gave my phone a shake to switch the shooting mode to "selfie", and with my flat hand started rhythmically thumping on my breastbone in time with the drumbeat of the nutcrackers. Just in case that wasn't enough, I beatboxed for all I was worth, making popping, clicking and drum-rolling noises I'd had no idea were even possible to produce with my tongue and lips. Then I raised my phone up high, lining it up so all the drummers were in the shot, and pushed the button.

There was a shrill scream from the elf lady. I swung around. She staggered back from Tom; the elf lord snatched his hand from his shoulder and veered away. Both of them were shrinking, shrivelling into themselves—all the elves were. The perfect green meadow faded and darkened to a muddy brown, and a roaring sound came from the white silk pavilion, which slowly collapsed in on itself, turning grey and ragged.

Tom sprang to his feet and ran back to me.

"You did it!" he cried. "Come on, quick!"

He grabbed me by the hand, and together we rushed away from the disintegrating meadow.

I threw one more glance over my shoulder. Where the beautiful illusion had been was only mud and chaos; small splotches of light with Dr.-Seussian outlines flitted back and forth across it.

In the middle of it all, a white-suited figure stood, swinging his hips to a tune only he could hear, his gaze turned towards to an invisible, adoring audience. Then once again, he looked up and right at us, gave a farewell wave, then faded away and I could see him no more.

We ran up the hill and rushed through the door of the crumpling hay shed, ducking in a hair's breadth before the lintel post came crashing down. It just clipped me on the shoulder as it fell.

And then we stood in Whitewell's dairy barn, surrounded by the sweet smell of cattle and feed and the soft sound of cows rustling and breathing. Behind us was a solid wall, to our right and left a few empty stalls. One of the cows turned her head, looked at us over her black-and-white shoulder, and gave a deep "Mooooh!"

Tom jumped, stared at the cow for a second,

then threw back his head and started laughing. He laughed and laughed until tears ran down his face.

I looked at him with a smile. "Care to tell me what's so funny?" I said when he finally caught his breath.

"Oh," he said, wiping the tears from his cheeks with the backs of his hand, "nothing much. Just the contrast from that—" he waved his hand in the direction of the barn's back wall, "—to *this*." He gestured at the cattle. "I've never been more glad to see a cow in my life!"

Abruptly he pulled me around to face him. "One more thing," he said, "and I'm not waiting another minute with this." He dropped to his knee in front of me and reached into his jeans pocket, still holding onto my other hand. "Mac, my darling, will you marry me?" In his fingers was the princess-cut diamond ring that I had last seen on the elf lady's hand.

My jaw dropped. "Where—how…"

He grinned. "You'd be surprised what a bit of grovelling can do. Puts you right in front of a lady's fingers. And if she's a cheat who's kidnapped you and tricked you into giving her a ring that was meant for someone altogether different, she deserves what she gets. So will you, my one and true love? You've brought them all to me: the partridge, the doves, the French hens…"

"… the calling birds, the gold rings, the geese,…"

"…the swans, the milking maids, the dancing ladies…"

"…and the leaping lords." I concluded. "But the pipers you delivered yourself."

"Not really. You caught them on screen." His

56

face was serious. "And the drummers are entirely to your credit."

"Mine and Eldon's," I said, gulping down a lump in my throat. "I'll never, ever…"

"…forget him? No. We owe him so much," Tom said. He squirmed on his knee. "But it's darn uncomfortable down here. So one more time: will you marry me?"

I held out my left hand, the fingers spread. "Get on with it already, Thomas Rimer. Of course I'll marry you—do you think I'd go through all that trouble for anyone but my true love?"

He slid the ring on my finger then, and stood up to give me a proper kiss.

The barn door creaked open and Celia wandered in, looking lost and defeated, her streaked grey hair hanging limply around her face and her eyes dull. But then she caught sight of Tom and me, and she whipped up her head, electrified.

"Did you see him?" she cried.

I nodded, and a light blazed up in her eyes. "Where? How?"

I turned and pointed behind us, and as I looked I saw a faint outline of a door in the back wall of the barn.

"Thank you!" Celia's hand closed on my forearm for just a moment, her face shining. She no longer looked her almost seventy years, but in a flash I could see the twenty-year-old she had been. "*Thank* you!" Then she rushed past me, her brown hair waving like a flag behind her—brown? Had I really seen that?—and she vanished through the door. For an instant, I saw a bright green spring meadow beyond, and then there was only a wall.

The real barn door burst open, and the oldest Whitewell girl came in, talking over her shoulder. "We have to get the cows done first," she said, "but as soon as we're done that, we'll get going on the search. We shouldn't be more than—" She turned around and saw us, and her jaw dropped. "What the…?"

Several more figures pushed into the barn behind her. There was Mary-Lou right at the front, Gina, Joe Engelhard—and they all stared at us as if they were looking at a pair of ghosts.

Mary-Lou was the first to find her voice. "What the heck are you doing here? And where have you *been* the last four days?"

Tom and I looked at each other. Four days? So it was January 5th—the Twelve Days of Christmas were over at midnight, over and done with.

"Where have we been?" Tom said, and he started laughing again.

"It's a long story," I said. "You'll find it hard to believe. It starts with a partridge in a pear tree…"

THE END

ACKNOWLEDGEMENTS

Many thanks to my beta readers, as always, Anna and Louise, and to the members of the Vernon Critique Group, without whom this little tale would not be what it is.

ABOUT THE AUTHOR

A. M. Offenwanger lives in rural Western Canada with her husband, daughter, sons, cats, dust bunnies, and a small stuffed bear named Steve. Christmas is her favourite time of year, and fortunately she has never encountered any elves to mess it up. Online she can be found on Facebook and Instagram, and on her website at www.amovitam.ca.